Nathan Saves Summer

Written by **Gerry Renert**

Illustrated by **Carrie Anne Bradshaw**

To Liz and Marcello with much love. *GR*

For my family and friends who have always supported me. *CAB*

Text ©2010 Gerry Renert
Illustration ©2010 Carrie Anne Bradshaw
Translation ©2010 Raven Tree Press

Renert, Gerry.

    Nathan saves summer / written by Gerry Renert; illustrated by Carrie Ann Bradshaw;
    —1 ed. —McHenry, IL : Raven Tree Press, 2010.

    p.;cm.

    SUMMARY: The story of a hippopotamus whose lifelong dream is to
             become the lifeguard for a small pond. One day an odd
             twist of fate allows him to achieve his dream.

English-only Edition
ISBN 978-1-934960-76-9 hardcover

Bilingual Edition
ISBN 978-1-934960-74-5 hardcover
ISBN 978-1-934960-75-2 paperback

Audience: pre-K to 3rd grade
Title available in English-only or bilingual English-Spanish editions

1. Animals/Hippos & Rhinos—Juvenile fiction. 2. Humorous Stories—
Juvenile fiction. I. Illust. Bradshaw, Carrie Anne. II. Title.

LCCN: 2009931225

Printed in Taiwan
10 9 8 7 6 5 4 3 2 1
First Edition

Free activities for this book are available at www.raventreepress.com

High up in the hills, there was a very,
very small pond. Most of the year,
it was as quiet as it could be.

4

But during the summer, it was as crowded and noisy as it could be.
That was when all the animals came for their summer vacations.
There were antelopes, monkeys, penguins, lions, zebras,
gazelles, hyenas, tigers, and giraffes.

And then there was Nathan the hippo, the largest animal for miles around.

The pond had everything the animals could ever want. It had lots of lounge chairs with umbrellas. It had a snack bar. It even had a cabana so the animals could change into their swimsuits. It had everything except for...

...a lifeguard.

At the beginning of every summer,
Nathan volunteered to be the pond lifeguard.
He demonstrated how long he could
hold his breath under water.

10

He showed everybody how many animals
he could carry at once, if he had to.

He even floated on his back,
becoming the perfect raft.

But every summer, the animals came up with
reasons why Nathan shouldn't be the pond lifeguard.
"Nathan, relax and enjoy your vacation."

"It's too hot to work all day."

"Next year you'll be the lifeguard."

This summer, though, Nathan was more determined than ever to be the pond lifeguard. He had saved money to buy every piece of equipment a lifeguard could possibly need.

14

He even put lots of sunscreen on his
nose, as every good lifeguard should.

STILL THAT WAS NOT ENOUGH.
The animals stared at Nathan.
Finally, one of the hyenas blurted out,
"Nathan, you can't be a lifeguard because…
you're just too LARGE."

Nathan sighed, "Maybe it's not me who's too large. Maybe it's the pond that's too small."

17

That night, Nathan worried that the other animals might be right.
Maybe he would never become a lifeguard because he was just too large.
Just then, he heard some loud splashing in the pond below and turned to look.

He saw one of the tiger cubs bobbing up and down in the water.

20

Nathan sprung into action.
Holding his brand new life preserver, he dove into the pond.
There was a huge splash.

Nathan held the cub securely with one arm.
He wiped the water out of his eyes with the other.

22

He looked around AND COULDN'T BELIEVE HIS EYES!

ALL THE WATER WAS GONE!
A crowd of animals gathered and stared
in disbelief at what was once their pond.

25

Looking upset, the tiger cub said, "Nathan, I was just trying to dive for a fish. You didn't need to jump into the pond." The giraffe sighed, "That's the end of our vacation. We'll never have summer here again."

Nathan now knew he would never become a lifeguard.
That night, he left the pond forever.

The next day, two penguins
were playing on the hill below
where the pond had been.
They noticed that all the water
had trickled down into a stream...

which flowed into a river...

28

which led to the most beautiful lagoon they had ever seen.
The penguins rushed back to tell all of the animals.

It wasn't long before the animals made
the lagoon their new summer swimming place.
Then, as loud as they could, everyone shouted,
"Nathan saved summer!" And they all ran into the water.
Nothing could have made Nathan happier!

30